PEDRO

PEDRO
GOES WILD!

by Fran Manushkin

illustrated by
Tammie Lyon

PICTURE WINDOW BOOKS
a capstone imprint

Pedro is published by Picture Window Books,
a Capstone imprint
1710 Roe Crest Drive
North Mankato, Minnesota 56003
www.capstonepub.com

Library of Congress Cataloging-in-Publication Data
Names: Manushkin, Fran, author. | Lyon, Tammie, illustrator. | Manushkin, Fran. Pedro.
Title: Pedro goes wild! / by Fran Manushkin ; illustrated by Tammie Lyon.
Description: North Mankato, Minnesota : Picture Window Books, [2019] | Series: Pedro | Summary: Pedro and his father go on a hike in the woods— where it turns out that Pedro knows a lot more about the plants and animals than his father does, but they both have fun anyway.
Identifiers: LCCN 2018054335| ISBN 9781515844501 (hardcover) | ISBN 9781515845638 (pbk.) | ISBN 9781515844525 (ebook pdf)
Subjects: LCSH: Hispanic American boys—Juvenile fiction. | Hiking—Juvenile fiction. | Fathers and sons—Juvenile fiction. | Forest animals—Juvenile fiction. | CYAC: Hispanic Americans—Fiction. | Hiking--Fiction. | Fathers and son—Fiction. | Forest animals—Fiction.
Classification: LCC PZ7.M3195 Pcd 2019 | DDC 813.54 [E] —dc23
LC record available at https://lccn.loc.gov/2018054335

Designer: Charmaine Whitman
Design Elements by Shutterstock

Printed and bound in the USA.
PA71

Table of Contents

Chapter 1
Take a Hike!

"It's a sunny day," said

Pedro's dad. "How about a

hike?"

"Cool!" said Pedro. "I love

the woods. We can be wild."

"Don't worry about getting lost," said Pedro's dad. "I'm a great hiker."

"Good!" said Pedro.

They began to walk.

"These leaves are pretty,"
said Pedro's dad. "Let's pick
some for Mom."

"Stop!" yelled Pedro. "That's
poison ivy."

"Wow!" said Pedro's dad.

"That was scary."

"Not as scary as bears,"
said Pedro. "I hope we don't
see any."

"Oh boy!" said his dad.

"If I saw a bear, I would try

flying away like that crow."

"That's not a crow," said

Pedro. "It's a hawk."

"He's fierce!"

said Pedro's dad.

"For sure," said

Pedro. "Hawks like

to eat rats."

"Yuck!" said Pedro's dad.

"I wouldn't!"

"Let's run now," said Pedro.

His dad ran fast. Suddenly

he yelled, "STOP! I see a bear!"

The bear was . . . a sweet,

fuzzy dog!

Pedro's dad laughed and

laughed. So did Pedro.

Chapter 2

Picnic Panic

"Now, let's eat," said

Pedro's dad.

"Your peanut butter

sandwich is terrific," said

Pedro. "Now, I need a drink."

"Uh-oh!" said his dad.

"I forgot to fill the canteen."

Pedro asked, "Dad, did you
ever hike before?"

His dad smiled. "A long
time ago."

"Let's give these ants a
sandwich," said Pedro.

The ants ate all of it. They
didn't need a drink.

They began walking again.

"Yikes!" yelled Pedro's dad.

"Something big just jumped

on my leg."

He ran in a panic and fell

in a puddle!

"It's only a frog," said

Pedro. "It can't hurt you."

"Oh my!" His dad laughed.

"I am a terrible hiker."

Chapter 3
Here Comes a Storm!

Pedro looked up at the sky.

"Uh-oh," he said. "A storm

is coming! Let's hurry home."

"We came on this path,"
said Pedro's dad.

They began walking. It was
the wrong path! Lightning
started! And thunder!

"Don't worry!" said Pedro.

"I think I know the right way.

But I can't run as fast as you.

Can you carry me?"

"Sure I can," said Pedro's

dad. He began running.

Uphill! Then downhill!

And uphill again!

Pedro's dad was strong and

fast. He ran like the wind.

"Go, Daddy!" yelled Pedro.

At home, Pedro's dad said,

"I'm sorry I didn't know much

about hiking."

Pedro shook his head.

"Dad, you know the most

important thing."

"What's that?" asked Pedro's dad.

"You know how to have fun!" said Pedro.

"I do!" His dad beamed.

They hugged on it.

About the Author

Fran Manushkin is the author of Katie Woo, the highly acclaimed fan-favorite early-reader series, as well as the popular Pedro series. Her other books include *Happy in Our Skin*, *Baby, Come Out!* and the best-selling board books *Big Girl Panties* and *Big Boy Underpants*. There is a real Katie Woo: Fran's great-niece, but she doesn't get into as much trouble as the Katie in the books. Fran lives in New York City, three blocks from Central Park, where she can often be found bird watching and daydreaming. She writes at her dining room table, without the help of her naughty cats, Goldy and Chaim.

About the Illustrator

Tammie Lyon began her love for drawing at a young age while sitting at the kitchen table with her dad. She continued her love of art and eventually attended the Columbus College of Art and Design, where she earned a bachelor's degree in fine art. After a brief career as a professional ballet dancer, she decided to devote herself full time to illustration. Today she lives with her husband, Lee, in Cincinnati, Ohio. Her dogs, Gus and Dudley, keep her company as she works in her studio.

Glossary

beamed (BEEMD)—smiled widely

canteen (kan-TEEN)—a small portable metal container for holding water or other liquids

lightning (LITE-ning)—a flash of light in the sky when electricity moves between clouds or between a cloud and the ground

panic (PAN-ik)—a sudden feeling of great terror or fright, often affecting many people at once

poison ivy (POI-zuhn EYE-vee)—a shrub or climbing vine with clusters of three shiny, green leaves. Poison ivy causes an itchy rash on most people who touch it.

terrible (TER-uh-buhl)—very bad

terrific (tuh-RIF-ik)—very good or excellent

Let's Talk

1. Who was better at hiking in the story? Explain your answer.

2. Pedro has a little brother named Paco. How would the story have been different if Paco had gone hiking too?

3. Do you think Pedro and his dad's day was a good day or not? Share details from the story to explain your answer.

Let's Write

1. Thinking about the story, list at least five reasons why people enjoy hiking.

2. Draw a map of hiking trails. Name your trails and include labels.

3. Pedro's dad thought a dog was a bear. Imagine they really did see a bear. Write a paragraph about what happens next.

JOKE AROUND

🍁 Which side of a tree has the most leaves?
the outside

🍁 Why did Humpty Dumpty have a great fall?
Because he enjoyed all the colorful leaves while hiking.

🍁 What did the hikers call the bear with no teeth?
a gummy bear

🍁 Have you heard the joke about the skunk and the hiking trip?
Never mind—it really stinks.

🍁 Why was the pine tree sent to its room?
It was being knotty.

🍁 What did the lake say to the hikers?
Nothing, it just waved.

🍁 Knock, knock
Who's there?
Woods
Woods who?
Woods you like to go for a hike?

🍁 Why are people who go hiking on April Fools' Day so tired?
Because they just finished a 31-day March.

HAVE MORE FUN WITH PEDRO!

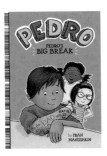